Dear Doris
To a great new friend!

Ern Hood

Copyright 2006 by Sheri Hood: 32749-HOOD
Library of Congress control Number: 2006905168
ISBN: 978-0-9793823-0-7 Hardcover

Printed in Hong Kong

This is a work of fiction. Names, characters, places and incidents either are the
product of the author's imagination or are used fictitiously, and any resemblance
to any actual persons, living or dead, events, or locales is entirely coincidental.

To order additional copies of this book, contact:
StonesThrow Publishing, LLC
www.thefearfulfairy.com

The Fearful Fairy

story written by
Sheri Hood

illustrated by
M. Faith Shaheen

To Joe Farago

Once upon a fairy time,
In the Land-of-Pixie,
Lived a little fairy girl
Everyone called Dixie.

And as you know, when fairies fly,
They're graceful, light and fair.
They dance and dart and somersault
And ride the summer air.

But Dixie was not like the rest.
The tale is sad but true.
The other fairies had four wings
And Dixie, only two!

Well, this was very troublesome
'Cause every time she'd fly,
Her wings would get all tangled up
Whene'er a breeze went by.

"A-poof!" the wind would whisper,
And in that very spot,
Dixie's wings would tie themselves
Into a granny knot!

The ants and bees, they tried to help,
But every time she flopped.
She'd only make it inches up
Before her bottom dropped!

"I *can't* fly, it's too scary."
She muttered to herself.
"Why was I born a fairy?
I'd rather be an elf!

Elves haven't any wings at all
And so they are at ease
To sit around and whittle sticks
And do just what they please!

Perhaps if I look to the sky
And tell a star my dream,
I can become an elf myself
All curly-toed and green!"

But morning saw no change at all
(Although she wished like crazy)
And with a tear she tucked her wings

And hid behind a daisy.

About that time a bumblebee,
Bumbling overhead,
Smelled a honeysuckle scent
Beside the garden shed.

And hopeful for some nectar sweet,
But prone to dart and dither,
He overshot the flowerbed…

And landed in the river!

Splash! Went the clumsy bumblebee,
Which was not good for him,
'Cause everyone in Pixie Land
Knows bumblebees can't swim.

"Help me, help me, someone please!"
The bee was calling out,
And from her daisy Dixie heard
His faint and distant shout.

Miss Dixie did not hesitate.
She bent her little knee,
And scuttled up into the sky
To look down for that bee.

But then, alas, when looking down
Her head began to spin.
The flowers were so tiny!
The air so light and thin!

Her heart began a'fluttering.
Her throat began to freeze.
Her wings were getting weaker
And twisting in the breeze!

Even mighty army ants,
Marching on their mound,
Saw Dixie struggling overhead
And scurried underground!

Dixie thought of giving up.
How simple it would be!
Until she spied that little bug
Now drifting towards the sea.

And saddened by his awful luck—
Not thinking of her own,
She made a choice right then and there.
She'd bring that poor bee home!

Suddenly her wings had strength
She hadn't felt before,
And even though she had but two
It felt like she had four!

And like a bird, her wings uncurled
To catch the wind just right,
And then, ta-da! She did not fall,
But was, at last, in flight!

Then swooping down above the bee
And right before he sank,
She grabbed him by his fuzzy stuff
And plopped him on the bank.

Of course the bee, quite happily,
Would soon tell all who cared

About the fearless fairy
And how his life was spared.

And in the bee community
The news swept every street.
Young Dixie was a heroine
To every bee you'd meet!

"Oh please," said little Dixie,
When hearing of the buzz.
"It really wasn't anything…

It's what a fairy does!"

Special Thanks
To Our Family:

Dean
Olivia
Amanda
Joshua
Terra & Todd
Chad
Emma
Moms & Dads
Jackie & Peter
Beanie & Cookie

And To Great Mentors:

Tracy
Mark
Doris
Mr. Smith